5230 8086

THE HA-HA-HAUNTING
OF HYDE HOUSE

Don't Miss

#5

THE HA-HA-HAUNTING OF HYDE HOUSE

by Tony Abbott

illustrated by Colleen Madden

EGMONT
New York USA

EGMONT

We bring stories to life

First published by Egmont USA, 2013
443 Park Avenue South, Suite 806
New York, NY 10016

Text copyright © Tony Abbott, 2013
Illustrations copyright © Colleen Madden, 2013
All rights reserved

1 3 5 7 9 8 6 4 2

www.egmontusa.com
www.tonyabbottbooks.com
www.greenfrographics.com

Library of Congress Cataloging-in-Publication Data
Abbott, Tony
The ha-ha-haunting of Hyde House / by Tony Abbott;
illustrated by Colleen Madden.
p. cm. -- (Goofballs ; book 5)
Summary: A ghost-sighting at a creepy haunted house means the
Goofballs have a new silly mystery to solve.
ISBN 978-1-60684-446-5 (hardcover) -- ISBN 978-1-60684-447-2
(pbk.) -- ISBN 978-1-60684-448-9 (ebook)
[1. Mystery and detective stories. 2. Haunted houses--Fiction. 3.
Ghosts--Fiction. 4. Humorous stories.] I. Title.

PZ7.A1587Hab 2013
[Fic]--dc23
2012045966

Printed in the United States of America

Book design by Alison Chamberlain

To my neighbor Henri, the nearest
Goofball I know!
—T.A.

THE HA-HA-HAUNTING
OF HYDE HOUSE

Contents

1

The Scary Beginning

My name is Jeff Bunter, and I'm a Goofball.

In fact, I'm the first Goofball ever.

You can ask my friends Brian Rooney, Kelly Smitts, and Mara Lubin.

"Jeff Bunter?" they'll say. "Yeah. He's a Goofball. The first one ever."

Of course, Brian, Kelly, and Mara are Goofballs, too.

Together, we're the most awesome team of mystery solvers since mysteries were discovered.

Before mysteries were discovered, I don't know what people solved. Math problems, maybe. Luckily, they *did* discover mysteries, and now we're the best at solving them.

Take Brian, for instance. But don't take him too far away. We need him.

Brian invents detective gear so nutty it almost never works. Maybe that's because he's the second Goofball ever, so he's had lots of practice. He's also the second shortest Goofball ever.

Kelly is the first shortest.

But she makes up for it by keeping an enormous pile of yellow hair on her head. She also power walks everywhere and is very smart and serious.

Kelly's so serious that when you say, "Knock-knock," she'll say, "What are you knocking on? I don't see a door. Are you knocking on your head? Is that what's making that noise?"

Which just makes her a perfect Goofball.

Then there's Mara.

She's as tall as me and as skinny as a number-two pencil. But Mara isn't as yellow as a pencil. Sometimes she wears purple shoes, red pants, a blue shirt, a white scarf, a pink headband, and big green glasses.

In other words, a truly goofy outfit.

And me?

I'm an expert at spotting clues. I'm so good that I spot clues even where there aren't any.

I write them all in my cluebook, which is a handy little notebook detectives use to solve mysteries.

Completing the Goofball team is my pet corgi, Sparky. He's been our official Goofdog since he was a puppy and barked like this:

"Goof! Goof!"

Together the Goofballs solve mysteries. We're the best. We're *so* good, it's downright scary.

But little did I know last month that our next mystery would be both goofy *and* scary!

4

It started like this:

Swoosh! Whoosh! Vrrrm! Errrk!

No, it wasn't Brian racing through the halls to the school cafeteria. It was me, riding my mountain bike to the Badger Point Library.

It was the afternoon of Halloween. The Goofballs were between cases, so we were helping Mrs. Bookman, the librarian, put on her annual Halloween Fun Day for Toddlers.

The official Goofball definition of *toddler* is someone too short to reach a doorknob but not too short to reach a cupcake.

Even Sparky was invited to Fun Day.

I was biking as fast as I could when—*errrk!*—I screeched to a stop at the corner of Main Street and Putney Lane.

When you're a Goofball detective like me, your eyes are trained to see clues that normal people don't see.

First, I spotted a big bunch of pink
balloons coming out of the flower shop.
Then I saw a couple of lady legs
sticking out from under the balloons.

"Goof?" Sparky barked.

"I think so, too, Sparky. Definitely a clue to something." I watched the balloons and the legs bobble around the corner and disappear down the street. *Disappear* is a special detective word that means *vanish*.

I wrote it all down:

Pink balloons
Lady legs
Disappear down the street

I wrote down some other things I saw:

A red bird
A stick
Fluffy clouds

I wasn't sure whether those last things were clues to a mystery, but you never know.

"We don't want to be late for Fun Day," I said to Sparky. "I heard there will be candy corn cupcakes."

"Goof!"

I felt good about getting all those clues before there was even a mystery.

But I had no clue at all about what came next.

Because before too long, those fluffy clouds would turn dark, that stick would be wet, that bird would fly away, and our new case would go from super goofy to super scary!

2

The W-W-Word Game

When Sparky and I trotted through the library doors, the first thing we saw was a tiny girl with dangly red braids.

She was running away from Mara, and she had a half-eaten cupcake in each hand.

"Proving half of my definition of a toddler," I whispered to Sparky.

"Olivia! Please stop running!"
Mrs. Bookman called after her.
"There's pumpkin drawing next.
You can draw a funny face!"

Just as Mara moved up behind the
girl to try to slow her down, the girl
jerked to a stop.

"I like frunny fraces," the girl said.

"Then draw Jeff!" said a muffled
voice behind me. "His frace is super
frunny!"

It sounded like something Brian
would say. But when I turned, all I saw
was a big top hat sitting on a couple of
shoulders.

"Brian? Is that you under there?
You're not supposed to dress up until
tonight."

Pop! Brian pulled off his top hat.
"Dad said I could wear his old tuxedo
for trick-or-treating. I'm trying his hat
on for size."

"It's too big for you," said Mara,
blinking at him through her big green
glasses.

"Except that the world knows my brain is bigger than a normal brain," said Brian. "So I thought the hat would fit. But it keeps falling over my ears."

"You should have big yellow hair like me," said Kelly, hustling through the door, wearing an orange sweatsuit and swinging her arms like a couple of helicoptors. "Mmm, candy corn cupcakes. I love them!"

"I don't," said Brian. "I heard that if you eat too many, a cornfield grows inside you."

Kelly was about to answer back, when someone's phone buzzed like an alarm clock.

Zzzz!

We spun around to see a woman say to the red-haired girl, "I'm sorry, Olivia. Grammy needs us. We have to go."

The little girl looked close to tears, until Mrs. Bookman offered her more cupcakes.

"I'm free!" she said, holding up three fingers and taking three cupcakes. Then she ran out the door with her mother.

"And I'm free," said Mara, "of having to chase her all around. That girl likes to run."

Mrs. Bookman waved her arms. "Now, everyone, it's pumpkin-drawing time!"

The toddlers cheered with delight.

Their drawings were pretty goofy, but Brian's was even goofier. He said he was drawing a "frunny frace," but his top hat kept falling over his eyes, so he couldn't see.

"I have an idea for you, Brian," said Mrs. Bookman. "Here are some old newspapers to stuff into your hat—"

"Newspapers!" Kelly gasped. "I love old newspapers. Old newspapers are history. Plus they're great for finding clues. Are you sure you want them close to Brian's brain?"

"It's all right," said Mrs. Bookman. "These papers are three years old. They're all on computer now, so we're recycling them."

"Can you recycle Brian?" I joked.

"If you did, I'd come back as Abraham Lincoln," he said. "Then my top hat would finally fit!"

Which is funny because Abraham Lincoln always wore a top hat like Brian's.

Next, everyone lined up to toss bean

bags into a plastic pumpkin. But every time someone threw a bag, Sparky jumped up on his hind legs and caught it.

Then he ran away with the bags.

"Now, children," Mrs. Bookman said, "we'll start word games in a minute. But first does anyone have a scary story to tell?"

"Me!" I said, because I love telling stories.

"Make it super scary!" said the kids.

Kelly and Mara turned the lights down low, while Brian sat behind me to make spooky noises.

"Gather around, people," I said in my deepest, scariest voice.

Then I started.

"It was a dark and windy afternoon."

"Whoosh, whoosh!" said Brian.

"Thunder thundered!"

"Boom-ba-boom!" said Brian.

All the toddlers' faces were turned to me. Their eyes were wide; their mouths hung open. I could tell they were getting scared.

Then I remembered. I love scary stories, but I don't like scary endings.

I like goofy endings better.

So I said, "And the door of the haunted house squeaked like a fuzzy dog toy!"

Just as Brian squeaked like a dog toy, the library doors banged open and our classmate Joey Myers rushed in. (His mom runs the flower shop I had seen the balloons walking out of.)

Right now Joey was shaking from the laces on his sneakers to the lashes on his eyes.

"Joey, what's wrong?" asked Mrs. B.

"I'm sc-sc-sc—"

"Word games!" said Mara. "We're starting word games! Are you . . . sc-sc-*scrambled*? Are you *Scandinavian? Scottish? Scatterbrained?*"

"I'm sc-sc-*scared*!" Joey cried.

Mara grumbled. "I was going to guess that next."

"Why are you scared?" asked Kelly.

Joey shivered. "I just saw a g-g—"

"My turn!" said Brian. "G-g-*golf course? Groundhog? Green pepper?* Wait. Not a . . . g-g-*gorilla?*"

"No!" said Joey. "I just saw a . . . g-g-*GHOST*!"

3

To Believe ... or Not

"Ghost! Ghost! Ghost!" the little kids screamed. Then they grabbed cupcakes and ran in circles until Sparky and Mrs. Bookman herded them back to their parents.

I stared at Joey. "A ghost?"

"Probably not," said Kelly.

Mara's eyes got big. "A ghost?"

"Doubtful," said Kelly.

Brian scratched his head. "These newspapers are itchy. Wait, a ghost?"

"A GHOST!" said Joey. "Ten minutes ago!"

"I don't believe in ghosts," said Kelly.

"I do," said Brian. "They're just people. Well, they're sort of *ex*-people. But still."

"I believe in ghosts," said Mara. "That's because I saw a ghost once. It was at night and from a distance and I didn't have my glasses on and I may have been asleep. But I'm positive I saw one.

"Since then, I've watched lots of cartoons with ghosts in them, so I've become an expert on Ghostology. That's what they call the study of ghosts."

"I'm not sure about ghosts," I said. "I like to keep an open mind."

"I used to do that, too," said Brian. "But one day it rained and everything got soggy in there, so now I keep it closed."

"Well," said Joey, "the ghost I saw was a great big blobby thing. It floated right across the ceiling of a haunted house!"

I yanked out my trusty cluebook.

Because this was a brand-new case, I flipped to a brand-new page. "Joey, please tell us where you saw this ghost."

"At the big empty house on the corner of Chestnut and Maple Streets."

I wrote that down. "Okay, Joey, go on."

"My parents just went to look inside and I went with them. They're thinking of buying it to open a bookstore there."

"I love bookstores even more than candy corn cupcakes," said Kelly. "I especially love *open* bookstores!"

"Everyone does," said Mrs. Bookman, coming over after the toddlers were settled again. "I know that old house. It's been empty for years. It's called Hyde House, because Lavinia Hyde used to live there."

"Spooky name," whispered Mara. "Write that down, Jeff."

Brian chuckled. "Does Lavinia Hyde have a friend named Lavinia Seek?"

"I wish she did," Mrs. Bookman said. Then she whispered, "It's been many years since anyone even saw Lavinia Hyde!"

"You mean, she *vanished*?" said Mara.

"No one knows," Mrs. Bookman said.

Vanished is a special detective word that means *disappeared*.

"There aren't any ghosts," said Kelly. "But if Joey saw something weird, it's a mystery. And a mystery is a case for the Goofballs."

I wrote that down because it sounded so good. "Joey, please tell us everything from the very beginning."

Joey gulped. "Well, I think the universe started as a big empty place. . . ."

"Not *everything*, everything," said Brian. "Just about the Haunting of Hyde House."

"Which is a great title for this case," Mara said, nudging me to write it down, so I did.

Joey blinked. "First my parents and I heard thumping. Then moaning like this—*Ohhhh!* Then we went through a bunch of rooms into a place called a parlor. Then we saw it. A white ghost floating across the ceiling. We all ran out of there. I won. But now my dad says our bookstore will never open!"

"Your dad should put a door on the house," Mara said. "That will make it easier to open."

"It *has* a door!" Joey said. "In fact, it has more doors than there are rooms to go into—"

"Stop!" said Brian. "Did you say doors?"

Joey nodded. "There are tons of—"

"Stop!" Brian said again. "I need to think."

He slowly paced the room. Sparky followed at his heels. They both stopped at the same time and spun around to us.

"Maybe it's all these newspapers near my brain, but I've figured the whole thing out," he said.

"Already?" asked Mrs. Bookman.

"Joey, you or your parents must have opened the wrong door," Brian said. "You opened the wrong door and—*fwit!*—a ghost flew out. People open wrong doors all the time and—*fwit!*—ghosts fly out. It's a national problem."

"Is it?" said Kelly with a frown.

Joey shivered. "Lavinia Hyde must be the blobby ghost I saw. Either way, we're not opening any bookstore now!"

Mrs. Bookman sighed. "I *so* wanted Badger Point to have its very own bookstore."

My mystery radar poked out of my mystery mind and started to buzz as I reread the clues.

Lavinia Hyde
Vanished
Haunted house
Blobby ghost!

I glanced at my fellow Goofballs.

Mara gave me a little nod.

Brian's hat gave me a little nod.

I looked at Kelly. "What about you, Kelly?"

"Well," she said, "a mystery is a mystery. And a Goofball is a Goofball. So, yeah."

And Kelly gave me a little nod, too.

"I declare right now," I said, "the Goofballs will go to Hyde House. We'll find this ghost."

"Or whatever scared Joey," said Kelly.

"And Badger Point's first bookstore will open its doors!" said Mara.

Joey shivered. "There sure are a lot of them in there. Doors, I mean."

4

Ghost-Hunting Gear

By the time we agreed to meet at my house and Sparky and I left the library, the fluffy clouds had turned gray.

A storm was coming.

"Great," I said to Sparky. "A haunted house in a storm. I don't know how this will end, but I hope it's not scary!"

I got the shivers just thinking about it. But as Kelly just said, a Goofball is a Goofball.

"Ghost or no ghost, Sparky, we have a brand-new case!"

"Goof! Goof!" he barked, bouncing home on his hind legs.

✻ ✻ ✻

Mom didn't bounce so much when I told her. "You're going where? To find what? When?"

"A haunted house. A ghost. Tonight, on Halloween," I said.

Mom gave me a look. "Um . . . no."

"But, Mom," I said, "I promised we would."

"But, Jeff," she said, "what if you go into that haunted house and never come out?"

"Mom, that's not going to—"

"I mean, I *guess* I could move my sewing machine into your room," she said. "Maybe the TV. And my computer and a small sofa. But what would I do with all *your* stuff?"

I nearly choked. "Mom!"

"I'm kidding," she said, giving me a hug. "But I think Joey and Joey's mother and Mrs. Bookman and I will go with you."

I sighed and shook my head slowly.

"Mom, Mom, Mom . . ."

"Yes, yes, yes?"

"We're professional detectives," I said. "Not to mention professional Goofballs, which, believe me, is really hard *not* to mention. You and the other ladies and Joey are just not goofy enough."

It was a great speech. It was almost *too* great. I watched my mom's face go through a hundred expressions until I thought she was going to say, "Fine. Just help me move my sewing machine—"

Luckily, she didn't.

"We'll wait in the car outside Hyde House while you and the Goofballs go in and find your ghost."

That made me feel a lot better, but I couldn't say that, of course.

I'm a tough professional.

"I guess you can be there," I said.

"I guess so, too," she said. "Now, please call your friends and ask them to get their parents' permission, too."

So I did. Then I rummaged in my closet for the blackest jeans and blackest sweatshirt and blackest sneakers I could find.

"I want to blend into the shadows," I told Sparky. "To hide from ghosts if I have to."

"Goof?"

"But, Sparky, you don't need a disguise. You're already wearing a fur coat!"

Then the doorbell rang, and Kelly power walked in. "You'll blend in with the shadows," she said when she saw my outfit.

"You'll blend in with . . . yourself," I said. "Kelly, you're wearing the same orange sweatsuit you wore at the library. We're hunting a ghost. You need to be ready!"

She made a face. "I *am* ready. Ready for nothing. Because I don't believe in ghosts."

"Suit yourself," I said.

"I did," she said. "I *sweatsuited* myself."

Next to come in was Mara.

She posed for us in a dark-blue outfit, from a pair of dark-blue shoes to two dark-blue chopsticks in her hair. On her belt hung a dark-blue flashlight.

"I'm all dark blue," she said.

"Stylish," I said.

Brian surprised us all by coming to the door in his dad's entire baggy tuxedo.

"How is that a ghost-catching outfit?" Mara asked him.

Brian grinned. "My dad says dress nicely, and you'll get in anywhere. A tuxedo is the best outfit for that."

"But Joey's mom has a key to Hyde House," I said. "Where else are you going?"

"It's simple," he said, which we knew meant it wouldn't be. "Hyde House has already made Lavinia Hyde into a ghost, right?"

"Probably not," said Kelly, twisting the ends of her big yellow hair.

"So . . . ," Brian went on, "if, say, *Kelly* gets made into a ghost, we might have to visit the land of ghosts to bring her back."

"Ghostology experts call it Ghostville," said Mara. "Jeff, write that down."

I did.

"If I have to enter Ghostville," Brian said, "I'll be dressed for it. Plus Dad's tuxedo is big enough for all my ghost gear. See?"

Then he showed us what he had in his pockets. It took so long we had to sit down.

He had: a tissue box, a yo-yo, a giant magnifying glass, a tiny harmonica, a compass, five colored toothpicks, four index cards, a clown nose, a butterfly net, a dozen paper clips, and a hard-boiled egg.

Kelly grumbled, "If ghosts *did* exist, which they don't, they would have the ability to vanish whenever they want. Not even that stuff would catch them."

"Don't worry," said Brian. "As a backup, I'm letting Sparky use my flashlight." Then he attached a tiny flashlight to Sparky's collar.

"All right, Goofballs," I said, "let's march!"

Which no one really did because my mom drove us.

Ten minutes later we were staring up at Hyde House. There was a big old gnarly tree growing in front of it. Through the branches, the windows stared down at us like creepy eyes, watching everything we did. On top, there was a spooky crooked tower.

"If I were a ghost," I said, "this is where I'd live."

"There are no ghosts," said Kelly. "But if there were, I'd agree with you."

"I guess we should go in," I said.

"I guess we should," said Brian.

"I agree," said Mara.

"That settles it," said Kelly. "Here we go."

But no one moved.

Whoosh, whoosh! Boom-ba-boom!

No, it wasn't Brian making noises this time. It was real wind howling and real thunder thundering. Then it started to rain.

"Better get inside before Jeff's open mind gets all soggy," said Brian. "Believe me, it's not a pretty sight."

On the top step we turned to the street. My mom sat in our car. Joey and his mother were in the backseat with Mrs. Bookman.

We all waved. Even Sparky waved his paw.

Then I drew in a deep breath, put the key in the lock, turned it, put my hand firmly on the doorknob, and pushed.

Eee-ooo-rrr-eee!

The door really squeaked like Sparky's fuzzy squeeze toy.

But nobody was laughing when we stepped into Hyde House.

5

The Vanishing Goofball!

Just as the front door started to shut behind us, Mara twirled around and caught it.

She pulled a chopstick from her hair and placed it between the door and the frame.

"We want to be able to run out of here if the ghost attacks us," she said.

"Good idea," said Brian. "It took me a whole hour to get out of my house once."

We all looked at him.

"Did you forget where the door was?" Kelly asked.

"No. I knew where it was."

"Then why did it take you an hour to get out of your house?" Mara asked.

"My mom wouldn't let me play outside until I finished my homework," he said. "It took me a whole hour."

As we stared at Brian, I realized that he was talking extra goofy because he was scared.

I realized that I was scared, too.

"Flashlight time," said Mara. She flicked on her blue one, but I guess it was mostly for style, because it didn't light up very much.

"Sparky," I said. He trotted over and I flicked on his collar light, too.

Brian took out his big magnifying glass. "Now let's bust some ghosts!" he said.

As Sparky sniffed around and his tiny collar light moved with him, we made out a big room. It was old and dusty. A few pieces of furniture—a chair, a floor lamp, a short table—were all covered with sheets.

"They look like ghosts," said Mara.

"Sheets keep dust off the furniture,"
I said.

"What's going to keep the dust off
us?" asked Kelly. "You know I'm
allergic. . . ."

She suddenly cupped her hands over her mouth and nose. "Ah . . . ah . . . *chooooooo!*"

Oooo . . . ooo!

We froze where we stood.

"The ghost!" Brian whispered.

"Or just an echo," said Kelly.

The echo faded. I took a deep breath. "Joey saw a blob in the parlor," I said. "Let's find the parlor."

We crept step by step to one door and opened it. There was another door behind it. We opened that. There, we found a hallway with a door at the end. We went through it.

"This house is a maze," said Mara.

"Ing," said Brian. "Amaz—ing."

Sparky snorted a sneeze. "Ah-Goof!"

"I'm going to draw the layout of these rooms," I said, opening my cluebook. "So we can find our way out. This house is scary."

"We have Joey to thank for that," said Brian. "Instead of a ghost he should have seen a green pepper, like I said in the word game. A green pepper is not scary at all. Plus if you eat one, it's good for you. But you know what's not good for you? A ghost. Especially a floating blobby one like Lavinia Hyde. . . ."

"Is . . . someone . . . there?"

A voice echoed from wall to wall and door to door, and we stopped dead.

"That was not a sneeze," I said.

"It's Lavinia Hyde!" whispered Mara.

"*I'm in here!*" the voice echoed.

We were just about to run out of the house when the thumping started.

Thump! Thump!

"Just like Joey heard!" Mara gasped. "It's coming from the haunted parlor!"

"It's probably just the plumbing," said Kelly.

"There is no plumbing!" I said. "No one's lived in this house for years. . . ."

Thump! Thump!

"Except the ghost of Lavinia Hyde!" cried Brian, heading back for the front door.

"Goofballs, look," Kelly insisted, grabbing Brian by the sleeve. "The only mystery is what Joey saw. And if we don't solve that, we may never get another case."

With that, she took Mara's
flashlight, yanked open the nearest
door, and marched into the darkness.
The door closed behind her.

I stared at Brian and Mara. "I don't know if Kelly's right, but we have to follow her."

"Not without a ghost-trapping trap," Brian said. "Good thing I brought a net with me."

Mara looked around. "Annette who? I don't see her."

"No, no," he said. "A net. I brought a *net* with me. Understand? A *net*!"

Mara frowned. "I still don't see her."

All at once, Kelly screamed a blood-tingling scream from behind the parlor door.

"Akkkkkk!"

"The ghost of Lavinia Hyde got her!" said Brian. He fell to his knees. "Don't let her take me! I'm too young to be an ex-person!"

We threw open the parlor door. Then the second parlor door. Then the third parlor door. Finally we were in the parlor.

And there it was. A white blob, floating across the beam of the flashlight Kelly was holding.

"Look!" Kelly said. "It's . . . it's . . ."

"*Now* do you believe in ghosts?" said Brian.

But the moment we tried to go to Kelly, the flashlight hit the floor and— *wham!*—so did we.

All at once, there was a puff of cold air, a tiny squeak, and a faint gasp.

By the time Mara picked up the flashlight, Kelly had vanished!

6

Interview with a Ghost

*V*anished!

As in *disappeared*!

We just froze where we lay on the floor. By the glimmer of the flashlight, we stared at the space that used to be Kelly.

"K-K-Kelly?" I whispered.

No answer.

We got up, took a step toward where Kelly had been, then fell down again. The flashlight went out again.

"What do we keep tripping over?" Mara asked.

"Sparky!" I called, and he trotted over and shone his light on a small chair, sitting right by the parlor door.

"A chair," I said. "Right by a door?"

"Everything is right by a door in this house," said Brian.

Mara started to wobble. "But . . . but . . . if Kelly vanished behind that door . . . that door must be the door to Ghostville! We have to rescue her!"

"Brian," I said, "straighten your tie. You're going in."

Brian shook his head and stepped back. "Uh . . . I like Kelly and stuff, but . . . I don't want to. I'm . . . sc-sc-*Scandinavian!*"

"Should I run and get my mom?" I asked.

Brian thought about that, then took a deep breath. "No. This is a mystery. Maybe it's way more scary than goofy, but if we don't solve it, we may not get another case."

Mara gasped. "That's exactly what Kelly said before she vanished!"

Brian's eyes went wide. "Maybe I'm channeling the ghost of Kelly!"

Mara gasped again. "That means she's still nearby. We need to do a séance!"

Brian tilted his head like Sparky does when he doesn't understand something. "Is a séance where you take a nap during the day? Because I could sure use a séance right now."

"That's called a *siesta*," I said.

"I thought *siesta* was a brand of iced tea," he said. "And you're not supposed to drink iced tea while you nap. You could drown."

"A séance," said Mara, "is where we call a ghost to talk to us from the world beyond. If the ghost of Lavinia Hyde took Kelly, we can try to get her back."

"We should try to get all of her, not just her back," said Brian. "If you leave her back back there, we'll have to go back for it—"

"Brian," I said, "calm down."

"But I'm . . . sc-sc-*scrambled*!"

I patted his shoulder. "We're all scrambled," I said. "Let's do a séance."

"First, we need a round table," Mara said. "I think I saw one a bunch of doors ago. . . ."

"Wait!" said Brian. "Let me set a trap in case Lavinia Hyde tries to grab someone else."

He slid the crumpled paper out of his top hat. "Jeff, write this down. I call it How to Trap a Ghost with a Newspaper."

I wrote down everything he did:

How to Trap a Ghost with a Newspaper

1. Take newspaper.
2. Separate pages.
3. Place them on the floor.

"What will that do?" asked Mara.

Brian sighed. "So many things. First, if the ghost comes for us, she'll walk over the newspapers and we'll hear her crunching them. That's called turning a *news*paper into a *noise*paper."

"Okay, but—" I started.

"Next," he said, "because Lavinia Hyde has been a ghost for so long, she hasn't seen the news. When she sees the *Badger Point News*, she'll stop to read it."

"Okay, but—" said Mara.

"Finally, the best part," Brian said. "When she's busy catching up on the news, we'll catch her. With a net!"

Mara leaned close to me. "Between you and me, I think 'Annette' is also a ghost."

We decided not to argue and left the parlor, heading toward the room with the table.

But the more I thought about it, the more Brian's newspaper thing bothered me.

Finally, I had to speak up.

"Look, is everybody thinking what I'm thinking?" I asked.

"Absolutely," Brian said. "Green peppers *would* be a great topping on a Goofball pizza."

"I'm talking about the ghost," I said.

Brian nodded. "They'd be a great topping on a ghost, too, but it would be hard to keep the pieces stuck on. On the other hand, if they fell off, Sparky would eat them. . . ."

"Goof!" said Sparky.

"No, look," I said, "the ghost of Lavinia Hyde floats. Ghosts don't use the floor. Not only that, but Kelly said they move through walls. So they don't use doors, either."

Brian looked unsure. "Meaning . . . what?"

"Meaning . . . I don't know yet," I said. "But this doesn't really make sense. We're missing something."

"Something called Kelly!" said Mara.

Then she opened a door and froze. "Oh!"

"What is it?" I said, peering over her shoulder.

"A bookcase," Mara said. "Kelly loved books."

"We'll get her back," I told her.

Mara nodded as she closed the door. "But I agree with Brian. We should get all of her."

Finally, we found the room we were searching for. We pulled a dusty old sheet off of the round table, then dragged four chairs to it. That's when I remembered that there were only three of us.

I wondered again if I should get Mom.

But Sparky said, "Goof?" so I patted the seat and he jumped into the fourth chair.

"Place your hands—and paws—flat on the table," Mara said. "Then spread your fingers and touch your thumbs together, like this."

Our six hands and Sparky's two front paws made a circle on the table.

Mara breathed deeply. "We have now formed an unbroken circle of spiritual energy. Kelly, if you can hear us, speak—"

Knock! Knock!

"Who's there?" Brian asked instinctively.

"It can't be Kelly," I whispered. "She doesn't do knock-knock jokes. It must be Lavinia Hyde!"

Then came a voice.

"Is . . . someone . . . there?"

Mara's eyes went wide. "You give Kelly back!"

"All of her!" I added.

Suddenly, there was a thump and a crash, and then we heard it.

The terrifying sound of . . . of . . . crunching newspapers!

7

Into Ghostville!

"Brian, your plan worked!" Mara gasped. "Lavinia Hyde *is* reading the newspaper."

"I'm not surprised," Brian said, clutching his ghost-catching net. "She must be hungry for news."

"Let's hope she's not hungry for anything else," I said.

Using my sketch of the house, and with Sparky hugging our heels the whole way, we tiptoed back through the rooms to the haunted parlor.

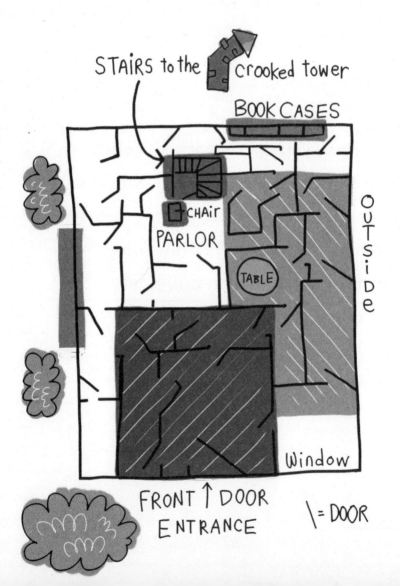

STAIRS to the crooked tower

BOOK CASES

CHAIR

PARLOR

TABLE

OUTSIDE

Window

FRONT ↑ DOOR
ENTRANCE

\ = DOOR

"Flashlights off," I whispered. "But get ready to turn them on."

I quietly turned the doorknob of the parlor door, while Brian raised his net overhead.

"If you touch me with that creepy ghost net, Brian, I'll turn *you* into a ghost!" said a voice.

And Kelly stepped out of the darkness.

"K-K-Kelly?" said Mara. "You're back!"

"And the rest of her, too!" said Brian.

I jumped up and down. "Kelly, what happened? What was it like in Ghostville? What do you remember about being a ghost?"

Kelly stared at us, then took Mara's flashlight and held it under her chin.

Spooky shadows moved over her face.

"Well," she began, "I didn't see all of Ghostville, of course."

"You weren't there very long," said Mara.

"Right," said Kelly. "But it's like a very old and very big—how do I say it?—*house*."

"Weird!" said Brian. "Jeff, totally write this down. We'll make millions! Kelly, what else?"

"Well, it has these things on every side of you," she said. "I guess you could say they're like—what's the word?—*walls*."

"Holy cow!" said Brian. "Houses! Walls! This is amazing stuff. Jeff—"

"I'm writing!" I said. "Kelly, go on!"

"With every step I took," Kelly said, "I put one foot in front of the other. . . ."

"And?" said Mara.

"I stepped on . . ."

"Tell us!" I cried.

"A floor!"

We were practically in shock, watching Kelly's face seem to float in the darkness.

"Finally," she said, "I reached out my hand. How do I say this . . . ? I *touched* something!"

We were all shaking.

"It must have been *sooo* creepy!" said Brian. "What was it? Don't tell us. No, tell us!"

Kelly swallowed once. Then again. She took a deep breath and finally spoke.

"A *doorknob*," she said.

Mara practically fainted. "Holy cow!"

I wrote down the words . . .

House
Walls
Floor
Doorknob

Then I realized what Kelly was telling us. "Wait a second. Are you talking about—?"

"This doorknob," Kelly said, tapping the knob behind her. "That's right. There's no Ghostville. I followed the blob through that door and couldn't find my way back."

Mara was shaking her head. "But we heard knocking. And the ghost even *spoke* to us. It said, 'Is someone there?'"

"That was me," said Kelly. "I said that. I banged on the walls, trying to find you. Which I finally did. And now I'm free!"

We all laughed, but my brain started to buzz when she said "free."

"Goofballs, we're getting close, very close. We keep coming back to this room. This parlor we're standing in right now is the scene of the mystery. Let's find clues!"

We did the famous Goofball search for clues. We each took a side of the room and looked and stared and studied everything.

Even Sparky went hunting.

But there weren't any clues except lots of dust and the single piece of furniture in the room. The chair.

"I still don't know why this chair is right next to the door," said Kelly.

"Or why it's the only furniture in the house that doesn't have a sheet on it," said Mara.

"Or why we didn't find an extra sheet lying around," said Brian.

That's when Sparky began licking the chair.

"Um, don't do that," I said.

But all at once, Kelly got down on all fours like Sparky. She stuck her finger on the chair where Sparky was licking and put it in her mouth.

"That's so gross," said Brian. "Why didn't I think of that?"

"Because you don't like candy corn cupcakes like Sparky and I do," Kelly said, licking her lips. "There's cupcake frosting on this chair!"

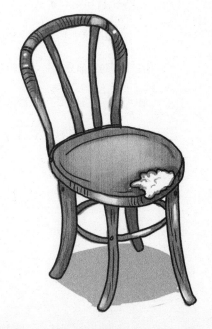

"And now I'm hungry," Mara said.

"Have an egg," said Brian, offering her his hard-boiled egg, which she popped into her mouth.

Meanwhile, my brain sparkled like a sparkler. "Right next to a door, there's a chair with no sheet on it but that's smeared with cupcake frosting. . . . I wonder . . ."

Then came another piece of the puzzle.

Crunch!

No, it wasn't another ghost catching up on news. It was Brian, trying to stuff the crumpled newspaper back into his top hat, when Mara stopped him.

"Hey," she said, her mouth still filled with egg, "thish papah's from eggzatly free yearsh ago, the day after Halloween."

It hit me like a bolt of lightning.

"Free yearsh ago!" I cried. *"Free?* Let me see that paper!"

Suddenly my mystery radar crackled like a big crackly thing, because I had found exactly what I was looking for.

"Goofballs," I said, "I have a hunch."

"It goes away when you shtand up shtraight," said Mara, swallowing.

I began to smile. "Goofballs, there isn't a single ghost in this house. There are three!"

"I need more gear!" said Brian.

"Only they're not really ghosts," I said.

"I still need more gear," said Brian.

"What do you mean?" asked Kelly.

"I mean only one kind of ghost needs a chair near a door or is a blobby floaty thing. The kind of ghost who's not even a ghost!"

"A ghost who's not even a ghost?" said Mara. "That's the scariest kind! Wait. No. But who's a ghost who's not a ghost?"

"We'll find out," I said, "as soon as we go through this door."

"Should I bring a net?" asked Brian.

"Sure," I said. "And tell her to be ready to sing."

"Sing what?" asked Kelly.

"You'll see," I said. "But I think we need Joey for this. Sparky?"

"Goof!" Sparky ran through the rooms. Five minutes later, he returned with Joey Myers.

"If I see a blobby ghost, I'm out of here," Joey said.

"You might see a blob," I said. "But no ghost. It's time to go on the offensive."

"I try never to be offensive," said Joey.

"Into Ghostville!" I said.

"Into Ghostville?" asked Mara.

"Into Ghostville!" said Brian.

"What's Ghostville?" asked Joey.

"A hallway," said Kelly.

And in we went.

8

The Goofy Ending

*E*rrrk! Errrk!

Behind the door we found a few more doors, but mostly we found a set of stairs.

I knew where they went.

Straight up to the crooked tower.

Every step creaked and groaned. The air got colder as we went upward.

I nudged Brian. "I know now that there aren't any ghosts," I whispered, "but I'm still sort of scared of creepy old houses."

"I know exactly what you mean," Brian whispered back. "I saw a movie once where a lizard was attacking a village, except that the captain of a boat had red shoes and two dogs but only one of them had spots."

I looked at him. "And the point of that is?"

"That the other dog didn't," he said.

And that's the thing about Goofballs.

I completely understood what Brian was saying. Not the part about the red shoes or the lizard or the captain or the dogs.

He was talking goofy so I would forget to be scared. And it worked.

There was one more door at the top of the stairs. "Here we are," I said.

It was time to enter the crooked tower.

"Now *I'm* scared," Brian said as we stood on the landing. "So scared I could throw up."

I decided to be extra goofy for him.

"Once," I said, "I woke up in the morning and I saw a thing moving around at the end of my bed. I jumped out, but it followed me wherever I went. I finally captured it. I still have it. Wanna see?"

Brian gulped. "Okay."

I picked up my foot. "It was this!"

Brian stared at my foot. Then at me. Then at my foot again. Then at his feet. Then he laughed. "That's a goofy story."

"I know, right?"

"We should go in together," said Kelly.

So together, we opened the final door.

And saw the ghost of Lavinia Hyde.

Except that the lady standing in front of us wasn't a ghost at all. Her snow-white hair was bunched up on her head. She had rosy cheeks and kind eyes and she smiled like a grandma.

Which is exactly what she was.

"You're not a blob at all," said Joey.

"Thank you," she said. "I try to keep fit."

"I'm having a fit right now," said Mara. "What? Who? Where? Why?"

"I'm Lavinia Hyde," the woman said. "I grew up in this house."

"I nearly *threw up* in this house," said Brian.

"But if you're not a ghost," said Kelly, "why are you haunting your own house?"

Lavinia Hyde smiled kindly. "My grandfather built the house with far too many doors. Since I left almost fifty years ago, I'd forgotten which door leads to which room. I wasn't haunting the house. I was lost in it."

"So was I for a while," Kelly said.

"You see," said Lavinia Hyde, "after we moved away from Badger Point, I never came back until my daughter's family moved here last year."

That's when the last pieces of the puzzle fell into place.

Or rather *walked* into place.

Because a door opened, and a little red-haired girl bounced in with her mother.

"We saw you in the library!" said Mara. "But you had to leave."

The girl's mother nodded. "My mom—Lavinia—called from the house and asked us to help her find something. Hello, I'm—"

"Julie Baker," I said. "Pleased to meet you."

She looked startled. "How did you know my name?"

I turned to Brian. "For that, I have to thank Brian's head."

"Most people do," he said. "Wait. Why?"

I asked for his top hat and slipped the newspaper out of it. "This newspaper from three years ago has a tiny piece about the birth of a girl named Olivia. Her parents are John and Julie Baker, and her grandmother is—"

"Lavinia Hyde!" said Mara. "I get it now!"

"Then who was the blobby ghost I saw?" Joey asked.

"Not *who*, but *what*." I turned. "Mrs. Hyde, we're ready to sing now. Will you do the honors?"

She frowned for a second, then smiled. "Yes!" She opened the door behind her and the blobby ghost floated out and up to the ceiling. Joey almost fainted.

Then she tugged on the blobby ghost, and a white sheet fell off to reveal a bunch of pink balloons. "I covered the balloons with the sheet because I wanted them to be a secret until the very last moment. Happy birthday, honey!"

"Oh, Grammy!" said Olivia.

"That's our cue!" said Kelly.

And we sang "Happy Birthday" to her.

Olivia's blue eyes twinkled. "Thank you!"

"Someone explain this to me before I almost faint again," said Joey.

"It all started with the first clues I wrote down this morning," I said.

Pink balloons
Lady legs

"The pink balloons told me it was a girl's birthday," I said. "I didn't think about them again until we saw all the sheets in the house. Hiding balloons under a sheet would look pretty blobby. It took me a while, but I finally put two and two together."

"Four, right?" asked Brian.

"Right," I said. "The next big clue came from Kelly's love of candy corn cupcakes."

"The frosting on the chair," she said.

"Also right," I said.

"But, Mrs. Hyde," said Mara, "why did you come back to Hyde House today?"

The woman smiled. "When I heard the house might be sold, I remembered that I had left behind some things I'd always wanted to give Olivia. My favorite books from when I was a child."

"People want to open a bookstore in your old house so they can find favorite books, too," said Kelly.

"A great idea," Lavinia Hyde said. "But I searched and searched, and I can't find my books. I've looked everywhere."

Mara practically jumped through the tower ceiling. "I know where those books are!"

"The case is not over!" Brian cheered.

"The *book*case is not over!" said Mara.

We all followed Mara down the stairs and through a million doors, until we stopped.

Mara opened one more door.

And there was the bookcase we had seen earlier. Lavinia Hyde went right over to it.

"Here they are. My childhood books. Here's *Ghoul Night, Moon* and *Make Way for Darklings*. And my favorite, *Scary, Scary Night*, by Vincent van Ghost! I love the pictures in that one."

Olivia bounced up and down when her grammy gave her the books. Sparky bounced up and down, too. We all did.

"The scary mystery was pretty goofy, after all," said Mara.

"My favorite kind," I said.

❌ ❌ ❌

One quick month later, with a little remodeling and a lot of dusting, Lavinia Hyde's old house became Badger Point's first bookstore!

"Goofballs," I said when everyone gathered in the book-filled parlor, "sometimes we discover mysteries. Sometimes mysteries discover us. But sometimes—just sometimes—we discover mysteries that turn into bookstores!"

Brian nodded. "It's all part of the Goofball theme song," he said.

"What Goofball theme song?" I asked.

"The one Sparky and I have been working on since we sang 'Happy Birthday' to Olivia. It uses the same tune. Ready, Sparky?"

I wrote down every word.

Even Sparky's part.

Oh, the Goofballs are . . . "Goof!"
And the Goofballs are . . . "Goof!"
So the Goofballs are . . . "Goof! Goof!"
Yes, the Goofballs are . . . "Goof!"

Which is pretty much the goofiest ending ever!

Meet the GOOFBALLS!

Jeff Bunter is the #1 original Goofball. Jeff was born to solve mysteries. He is in charge of keeping track of clues in his ever-present cluebook. He says that a private eye has to notice everything—because you never know what might be a clue!

Brian Rooney is Jeff's best friend. He's an inventor who loves to build crazy things that don't always work but that look really cool and help the Goofballs solve mysteries.

Mara Lubin is as tall as a fashion model, as skinny as a rake handle, and wears giant green glasses. She's also a master of amazing disguises.

Kelly Smitts is as smart as a computer, but she doesn't look like one. Unless a computer is really short, really suspicious, and has curly yellow hair.

Sparky is the official Goofdog. He's Jeff's scruffy Pembroke Welsh corgi, and he herds clues to help the Goofballs in every case. *Goof! Goof!*